Marge's Little Lulu
AND HER MA... KS

S... ER

NEW YORK

Special Package for this Little Golden Book

THIS IS A BRAND-NEW STORY, WRITTEN AND ILLUSTRATED ESPECIALLY FOR GOLDEN BOOKS

THE LITTLE GOLDEN BOOKS ARE PREPARED UNDER THE SUPERVISION OF MARY REED, PH.D.

FORMERLY OF TEACHERS COLLEGE, COLUMBIA UNIVERSITY

WELCOME TO LITTLE LULU

For a long time Little Lulu has been wondering how she would look in a Little Golden Book. Here, finally, she makes her bow and—of all things—as a magician.

It was a pleasant surprise to us to discover that Little Lulu knew how to make cute toys and other objects out of Kleenex tissues. It occurred to us that thousands of other children might want to make these, too, and so we asked the International Cellucotton Products Company how they would feel about making up for us a special pack of tissues for Little Lulu's book. They cheerfully agreed and we are properly grateful to them.

Have fun, and we hope that the things you make turn out beautifully.

—THE PUBLISHERS

LITTLE LULU wanted to be a magician, more than anything in the world. She had made herself a costume from her father's tail coat. He hadn't missed it yet. She even had a black moustache to wear.

Now all she needed was some tricks to do.
She had seen just the kind she needed in the
Magic Shop. So she was shaking out money
from her piggy bank to buy some. It looked
as if she had just about enough.

"Lulu! Little Lulu!" she heard her mother call. "Little Alvin is here to play."

"Humph!" said Little Lulu to herself. "How can a person get to be a great magician if she has to play with little kids all the time?"

Pocketing her money, she clomped down the stairs, with a scowl for Little Alvin.

"Hi, Lulu," Little Alvin beamed. "Let's go for a walk." He held out his hand.

"Okay," said Little Lulu, thinking to herself that she would steer him past the Magic Shop to buy her trick.

So off they started, hand in hand.

"Tinkle-tinkle-toora-loo!"
Around the corner came the ice cream man.
"Oh oh!" said Little Lulu to herself. But it
was too late. Little Alvin had spotted him.

"Ice cream! Ice cream!" he shouted, tugging at her hand. "Please, Lulu, please."

Lulu was so happy to hear him say Please that she dug into her pocket and bought two ice-cream bars.

Then, licking happily, on they went.
But soon little Alvin's toe struck a crack.
Su-plop! down he fell, ice cream and all.
"Wah!" he roared, stooping to try to pick
up the squashed and melting ice cream.

Little Lulu was more concerned about the ice cream on Alvin's foot. From her pocket she pulled a small pack of Kleenex tissues.

Then, soaking and sponging, she cleaned Alvin off as well as she possibly could.

"There!" she said when she had finished. "Isn't that fine?"

"No," little Alvin wailed. "Want my ice cream."

Little Lulu tried to be very patient with him. "I've already spent the money I'd saved for a magic trick," she explained.

But Alvin did not care. "Want my ice cream!" he roared. "Ice cream!"

"Lackaday," a strange voice broke in, a crackling little voice near Lulu's ear.

She turned to see a little old woman wearing a long black dress and cape, and leaning on a twisted walking stick.

"What's the matter, laddie?" the little
woman asked in a raspy little cackling voice.

"Want my ice cream," Alvin sobbed.

"Dear dear now," the little woman clucked.
"Isn't that too bad." For the ice cream man
was out of sight.

She wiped his eyes and helped him blow
his nose.

"Wouldn't this be as good as ice cream?" she asked then. And there, before Alvin's startled eyes, a small white rabbit wagged his ears.

"Hi," said the rabbit (or Alvin thought it did—it spoke in the little woman's voice). "What are you crying for?"

"Mine," said Alvin, reaching out. And the rabbit was in his hands.

"Here is a flower for the bunny to sniff," the little old woman said.

Sure enough, she held a pretty carnation out to him.

"Mine," said little Alvin happily.
"And how about a dolly?" the wonderful
woman asked. One, two, three, there it was.

"Why, it's like magic," Little Lulu cried. "That's what it is! Magic tricks! Could I learn to do them, do you suppose?"

"Of course, my dear," the little old woman smiled. She hobbled into her strange little house and brought back more Kleenex tissues. Soon Lulu knew all the tricks.

"Oh, thank you," said Lulu, waving a doll, as she and Alvin started home.

"Come again, dearies," their new friend smiled. "Ask your mother to let you come to visit some day, and I'll show you lots of wonderful things."

Lulu could hardly wait to go back. She did
her tricks for her mother and father, and they
were much impressed.

"I'll go with you, dear," her mother said one day, when they were out shopping. So Lulu led the way, straight to the spot where she and little Alvin had met their strange little friend.

The house was not there. There was no sign of a little old woman in a long black dress and cape.

Lulu could scarcely believe her eyes. But at last she thought she understood.

"Perhaps it all was magic," she said. And I guess perhaps it was.

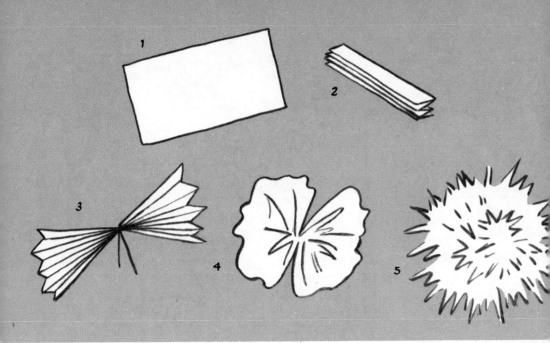

Would you like to learn these tricks too?
Here are the directions:

A Carnation for You

1. Take one folded sheet of Kleenex tissue.
2. Accordion fold as in the picture, starting at narrow end.
3. Tie at the center.
4. Open the folds out.
5. Shred the edges, and separate layers of Kleenex. Hold flower together, tie base, and fluff out.

Now your carnation is ready to wear!

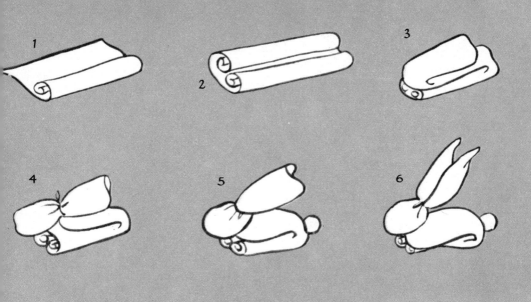

Need a Pet?

1. Roll a sheet of Kleenex tissue from one edge to the center.
2. Roll the opposite edge as shown.
3. Fold into three sections.
4. Tie the upper fold to make the head.
5. Tie the lower fold to make the tail.
6. Tear the top section to make the ears.

Now you can play with your bunny!

A Doll to Play with

1. Wad up a sheet of Kleenex tissue and put it in the middle of a second one.
2. Wrap the large sheet over the other, and tie.
3. Roll one sheet for arms.
4. Roll another for legs.
5. Tie arms and legs as shown.
6. Slip head and dress over arms and legs; tie as in picture.

Your doll is ready to play!